A Sweet Passover

BY **Lesléa Newman**

ILLUSTRATED BY **David Slonim**

SCHOLASTIC INC.

W9-AUC-593

Miriam loved celebrating Passover at Grandma and Grandpa's house.

She loved pinning a piece of lace to her hair just like Grandma did before she lit two tall candles and sang a special blessing to start off the *seder*.

She loved walking around the table with a towel draped over her arm while Mommy poured water from a white pitcher over everybody's hands.

She joyfully sang the Four Questions in Hebrew, and then listened as Grandpa read the answers from the *Haggadah* and told the story of the Jews' exodus from Egypt in his deep, booming voice.

She giggled at the way Daddy said, "Warm . . . warmer . . . hot!" as she got closer and closer to finding the *Afikomen* that he had hidden after he broke the middle matzah in half and tucked one of the pieces between two of Grandma's cookbooks high on a kitchen shelf.

She happily stood beside Aunt Rachel and Uncle Nathan
when they opened the front door to welcome Elijah the Prophet,
and she laughed when Bubbeleh joined them and howled at the
full moon.

Miriam loved everything about Passover, but most of all she loved eating matzah, and during the eight-day festival she ate as much of the unleavened bread as she could.

On the first day of Passover, Miriam and Grandma ate matzah with butter.

On the second day of Passover, Miriam and Grandpa ate matzah with jelly.

On the third day of Passover, Miriam and Aunt Rachel ate matzah with tuna salad.

On the fourth day
of Passover, Miriam and
Uncle Nathan ate matzah
with egg salad.

On the fifth day of
Passover, Miriam and
Mommy ate matzah with
cream cheese.

On the sixth day of Passover, Miriam and Daddy
ate matzah with cottage cheese.

On the seventh day of Passover, Miriam ate lots of matzah by herself. She ate matzah with almond butter and matzah with apple butter. She ate matzah with blueberry jam and matzah with strawberry jam.

She ate plain matzah, egg matzah, whole wheat matzah, and chocolate-covered matzah.

All week long, Miriam ate nothing but matzah, matzah, matzah.

When she woke up on the last day of Passover, Miriam was sick, sick, sick of matzah. All she wanted for breakfast was a thick slice of warm toast or a soft, chewy bagel or a sweet cinnamon doughnut or a freshly baked blueberry muffin. But Passover wasn't over until sundown, which meant that Miriam had to wait all day long before she could eat any of those things.

"Miriam," Grandpa called from downstairs. "Time for breakfast."

Miriam groaned and pulled the blankets over her head.

"Miriam?" Grandpa called again.

"I'm not hungry," Miriam called back.

"Are you sure?" Grandpa asked. "I'm making French toast."

"I'm coming!" Miriam jumped out of bed, dressed herself, and ran downstairs.

And there was Grandpa with an apron tied around his waist and a puffy chef's hat perched on his head.

"Good morning, *shayneh maideleh*." Grandpa gave Miriam a hug and a kiss on the *keppie*. "Ready for some French toast?"

Miriam looked at the counter where Grandpa had placed eggs, milk, butter, and a frying pan. "Where's the bread?" she asked.

"Bread? I can't use bread. It's still Passover," Grandpa reminded her. "That's why I'm using matzah."

"Matzah?" Miriam moaned. "How can you make French toast with matzah?"

"I'm making Passover French toast," Grandpa explained. "I'm making *matzah brei*."

"Matzah brei? Yuck." Miriam folded her arms. "I'm never eating matzah again."

"Never? That's too bad," Grandpa said. "You don't know what you're missing." And then he began to cook.

First Grandpa crumbled up the matzah and soaked it in warm water.

Next he cracked some eggs into a bowl, added a little milk, and beat the mixture with a fork.

Then he drained the matzah and poured the beaten eggs and milk over it. Finally, Grandpa sliced butter into a great big frying pan.

As soon as the butter began to sizzle, he poured in the uncooked matzah brei. When it was brown at the edges, Grandpa slipped his hands into a pair of oven mitts, placed a large plate on top of the frying pan, and flipped the whole thing over.

"Ta-da!" crowed Grandpa. "Passover French toast! Doesn't that look delicious?"

"No," said Miriam, wrinkling up her nose. "No more matzah for me."

"Suit yourself." Grandpa slid the matzah brei back into the pan to cook the other side. "Will you please set the table?"

Miriam took out the special Passover plates and put one at each place. Just as she set down the last fork and spoon, Mommy and Daddy and Aunt Rachel and Uncle Nathan and Grandma scrambled into the dining room.

Mommy spooned applesauce on top of her matzah brei. Daddy poured maple syrup over his piece. Aunt Rachel sprinkled her serving with sugar and cinammon. Uncle Nathan smothered his slice with sour cream. Grandma added salt and pepper to her matzah brei. Grandpa left his plain.

"*Essen in gezunt*," said Grandpa, picking up his fork. "Eat in good health. Enjoy."

"*Oy*, is that good," said Grandma.

"The best I've ever had," added Mommy.

"May I please have seconds?" asked Uncle Nathan.

"Save another piece for me," said Aunt Rachel.

"My compliments to the chef," said Daddy.

They were so busy eating, no one noticed that Miriam had nothing on her plate. Soon breakfast was over and all was quiet—until Miriam's belly let out a long, loud rumble.

"Miriam, didn't you get enough to eat?" Mommy asked.

"No," Miriam answered.

"Miriam is never eating matzah again," Grandpa announced to everyone.

Mommy and Daddy and Aunt Rachel and Uncle Nathan and Grandma all gasped. **"Never?"**

"Not even on Passover?" asked Mommy. "But, Miriam, we always eat matzah on Passover. How else will we remember that our ancestors were slaves in Egypt, and when Pharaoh granted them freedom, they had to leave in such a rush, they couldn't even wait for the bread dough to rise?"

"How else will we remember that even the plainest
food eaten in freedom tastes sweeter than the fanciest
food eaten in slavery?" Daddy asked.

"That's why we say, 'Have a *zissen Pesach*,'" Grandma told Miriam. "Have a sweet Passover."

"Matzah is such a simple food, it reminds us to be humble," explained Uncle Nathan. "It doesn't puff itself up, and we shouldn't puff ourselves up, either."

"It's a *mitzvah* to eat matzah," Aunt Rachel added. "A good deed. And just as the matzah was baked in a hurry, we should always be in a hurry to do a good deed whenever we can."

"Matzah goes with everything," Grandpa said. "And that reminds us that we should get along with everyone, too."

"And if all those reasons weren't enough for us, *dayenu*," Grandma said, "your grandfather happens to make the best matzah brei in the world."

Miriam looked around the table at each member of her family and thought over what everyone had said. Then she asked in her most humble voice, "Grandpa, will you please make me a matzah brei?"

"I'm sorry, Miriam," said Grandpa, patting his big, round belly. "I'm too full to cook."

"Please, Grandpa?" said Miriam. "Pretty please with applesauce on top?"

"No," said Grandpa. "I'm not going to make you a matzah brei."

"Why not?" asked Miriam.

"Because," said Grandpa, handing her an apron and a puffy chef's hat, "**we're** going to make a matzah brei together!"

Miriam crumbled up the matzah and beat the eggs while Grandpa melted butter in the frying pan.

Miriam poured the uncooked matzah brei into the pan and watched as Grandpa fried it up. When the matzah brei was ready, Grandpa set a great big piece in front of Miriam. "*Essen in gezunt, shayneh maideleh*," he said. "Eat in good health. Enjoy."

And Miriam did.

The Best Matzah Brei in the World

(as told to the author by her father)

This is a fun meal to make with the help of an adult. Always make sure an adult helps you when you are cutting items and using the stove or other hot surface.

This recipe makes one large matzah brei.

Ingredients

- **7 pieces of matzah**
- **warm water**
- **3 eggs**
- **$\frac{1}{4}$ cup milk**
- **pinch of salt (optional)**
- **2 tbsp butter**
- **toppings such as applesauce, sugar and cinammon, maple syrup, sour cream, and salt and pepper**

Utensils

- **large mixing bowl**
- **small mixing bowl**
- **2 large plates**
- **fork or whisk**
- **measuring cup**
- **mixing spoon**
- **frying pan**
- **spatula**
- **knife**

- Break up seven pieces of matzah into small pieces and soak in warm water in the large bowl for one minute. Then drain by covering the bowl with a large plate and tipping it to let the excess water run out.

- Using the fork or whisk, beat three eggs together in the small bowl with the milk and a pinch of salt (optional), and then add this mixture to the crumbled, drained matzah. Mix together well.

- In a large frying pan, melt the butter.

- Pour the matzah brie mixture into the frying pan. Spread it out evenly so that it resembles a large pancake. Cover and cook over a very low heat for about ten minutes, until crisp and brown on one side (raise the edge of the matzah brie with a spatula to check if it's crisp and brown).

- When the matzah brie is cooked on one side, turn it over by placing the other large plate over the pan and then flipping the whole thing over. While the matzah brei is on the plate, add more butter to the frying pan, if necessary. Then slide the matzah brei from the plate back into the pan to cook the other side. Again, cover and cook over very low heat for about ten minutes.

- When the second side of the matzah brei is crisp and brown, it is done. Cut into wedges and serve with applesauce, sugar and cinammon, maple syrup, sour cream, or salt and pepper. *Essen in gezunt!*

Author's Note

Passover (*Pesach* in Hebrew), also called the Festival of Freedom, is the eight-day Jewish holiday that celebrates the exodus of the Israelites from Egypt in approximately 1225 B.C.E.

The Israelites lived peacefully in Egypt for many years until a Pharaoh who despised them came into power and turned them into slaves. According to the Book of Exodus, the Lord ordered Moses to lead the Israelites out of Egypt. But Pharaoh wouldn't allow it. So God visited ten plagues upon the Egyptians: blood, frogs, vermin, wild beasts, pestilence, boils, hail, locusts, darkness, and slaying of the firstborn. Not until the final plague, when the firstborn sons of the Egyptians were slain, did Pharaoh allow the Jews to leave Egypt. (The Angel of Death passed over the homes of the Jews because they had been forewarned to smear their doorways with lamb's blood. Thus, the holiday is called "Passover.")

When Pharaoh told the Israelites to leave, they were in such a hurry, they didn't even wait for their bread dough to rise. Soon after they left, Pharaoh changed his mind and sent his army after them. When the Israelites came to the Red Sea, a miracle occurred: the waters parted so that the Israelites, led by Moses' sister Miriam, could escape the Pharoah's army.

Ever since then, Jews all over the world have celebrated Passover by eating matzah (unleavened bread) during the eight days of the holiday and enjoying a special dinner called a *seder* on the first and second nights of the festival. During the seder, the *Haggadah*, a book that tells the story of Passover, is read. There are many steps to the seder, including washing hands, eating bitter herbs, and hiding the *Afikomen*. Early on during the seder, three pieces of matzah are set aside. The middle piece is broken and one half of it, the *Afikomen*, is hidden. *Afikomen* means "dessert" in Aramaic, and the seder cannot be concluded until the *Afikomen* is found and shared by all. In some families, an adult hides the *Afikomen* and the children search for it. In other families, a child hides it and the adults search. In most families, whoever finds the *Afikomen* receives a prize.

Many families add customs or interpret existing rituals in their own way during the seder. For example, Miriam's family lights candles at the beginning of the seder to sanctify the day. Not every family does that. All members of Miriam's family wash their hands at the start of the seder. In some families, only the leader's hands are washed. There are many, many versions of the *Haggadah* to choose from. Some are very strictly traditional; others are not. The most important thing about the seder is that each participant finds it a meaningful experience.

Glossary

Afikomen: literally, "dessert"; the middle matzah, which is broken and hidden during the seder

Bubbeleh: literally, "little grandmother." This is a widely used term of endearment, akin to "darling."

Dayenu: literally, "It would have been enough for us." "Dayenu" is also the name of a song traditionally sung during the seder.

Essen in gezunt: Eat in good health.

Haggadah: a book that tells the story of Passover

Keppie: an affectionate term for head (derived from the Yiddish word *kop*)

Matzah: unleavened bread, traditionally eaten during Passover. It can also be spelled "matzo," "matzoh," or "matza."

Matzah brei: fried matzah

Mitzvah: a good deed; literally, "commandment"

Oy: a very useful and versatile word that can be an expression of surprise, joy, sorrow, pain, fear, or excitement

Seder: festive Passover meal

Shayneh maideleh: beautiful girl

Zissen Pesach: sweet Passover

For my father,
who makes the best matzah brei in the world!
—L. N.

To Claire Greenberg
—D. S.

No part of this publication may be reproduced, stored in a retrieval system, or transmitted in any form or by any means, electronic, mechanical, photocopying, recording, or otherwise, without written permission of the publisher. For information regarding permission, write to Abrams Books for Young Readers, an imprint of Harry N. Abrams, Inc., 115 West 18th Street, New York, NY 10011.

ISBN 978-0-545-70614-8

Text copyright © 2012 by Lesléa Newman. Illustrations copyright © 2012 by David Slonim. All rights reserved. Published by Scholastic Inc., 557 Broadway, New York, NY 10012, by arrangement with Abrams Books for Young Readers, an imprint of Harry N. Abrams, Inc. SCHOLASTIC and associated logos are trademarks and/or registered trademarks of Scholastic Inc.

12 11 10 9 8 7 6 5 4 3 2 1   14 15 16 17 18 19/0

Printed in the U.S.A.   40

First Scholastic printing, March 2014

The art in this book was created using acrylic and charcoal on illustration board.
Book design by Melissa Arnst and Maria T. Middleton